THE ORIGINS OF BUNNY KiTTY

A TALE FOR ALL AGES

STORY AND PAINTINGS BY:
DAVE "PERSUE" ROSS

MAGIC SPELL BY:
DIANE "MONNY" SATENSTEIN

GINGKO PRESS

Creative Direction & Editing: Dave "Persue" Ross

Written By: Dave "Persue" Ross & Diane Satenstein

Art Direction: Ellen Rutt

Special Thanks: Diane Satenstein (R.I.P.), Mildred Satenstein (R.I.P.), Penelope Ross, Alli Bautista, Todd, Heather, Peter, Nick and Emily Ross, the Ross family. Jesse Cory, Dan Armand, Pietro Truba, Roula David, Ellen Rutt and the 1xrun family. All the people that have given me the support I needed to get this out to the world. Thank you!

First Published in the
United States of America by:

GINGKO PRESS

Gingko Press, Inc.
1321 Fifth Street
Berkeley, CA 94710, USA
www.gingkopress.com

In association with:

1xRUN Editions
1410 Gratiot Ave.
Detroit, MI 48207
1xrun.com

ISBN: 978-1-58423-652-8
First Edition limited to 1750 copies
Artist Edition 750 copies

Printed in China
© 2016 PERSUE / BUNNY KITTY
BUNNYKITTY.COM

WE DID IT MOM!

DIANE 'MONNY' SATENSTEIN

NOVEMBER 6, 1946 - NOVEMBER 19, 2015

THE ORIGINS

In the beginning, in the country, there lived a little kitty cat named Daisy. Daisy lived with her mother and three brothers. Daisy and her brothers spent most of their days playing. Climbing trees, chasing after butterflies, pouncing on ladybugs, and taking catnaps in the tall grass was their daily routine. At night, fireflies sprinkled the dark sky with light. Daisy's brothers would leap towards the sky in an attempt to catch them, but Daisy would just sit quietly and watch the fireflies light up the night.

Early one evening, after an especially delicious dinner of clam croquettes, Daisy's mother informed her children that they were moving to the city to live with their grandmother. Daisy had never met her grandmother, but had heard wonderful stories about her. Daisy and her brothers danced around their mother shouting, "We're going on an adventure!"

And so plans were made. The family would travel by ferry to the city.

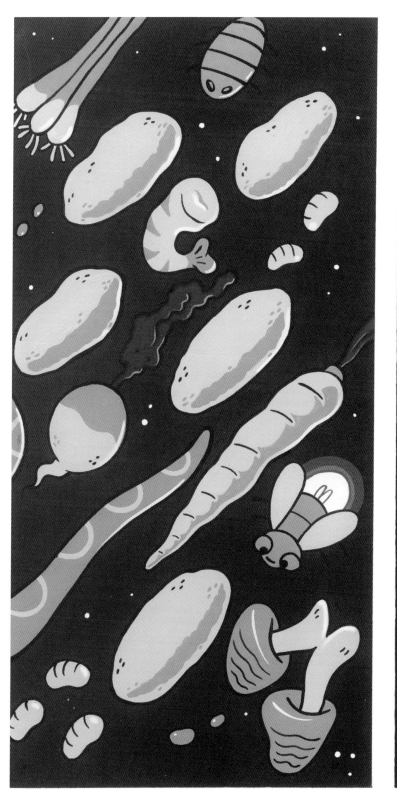

The day finally arrived for them to leave. As they were boarding the ferry, Daisy suddenly remembered that she had forgotten her beloved stuffed birdie, Twurp. As she sped over the rolling hills, she yelled back to her family, "I'll be right back!" Daisy's mother called for her. "Come back! Come back this instant!" But Daisy didn't listen to her mother.

Daisy ran straight to the secret nest she had made for herself and Twurp, when she wanted quiet time away from her brothers. Twurp was not in the nest.

Daisy scrambled everywhere, asking herself, "Now where did I put him?" Daisy took a deep breath and tried to think where she last played with Twurp. And then it dawned on her. She must have left him by her favorite tree last night when she was watching the fireflies. Daisy ran as fast as she could to the tree. And there was Twurp, just where she had left him.

Daisy grabbed Twurp and ran towards the ferry dock. She could see the puffs of steam over the rolling hills. And then she heard the horn. The ferry was ready to leave. She told herself to run as fast as possible.

It was difficult for Daisy to keep a fast pace. There were overgrown roots and holes where the water snake families lived, which made it hard for her to run. As Daisy approached the river, she saw that the ferry was leaving the dock. She could hear her mother yelling, "Hurry Daisy! Run faster!" Her brothers yelled "Jump, jump!" Just as she was about to jump she tripped over a big knotty root, and fell flat on her face. All she could see were stars. She heard faint echoes from her mother and brothers as they still called her name. Daisy was very tired.

She fell asleep.

When Daisy woke up, she didn't immediately remember what had happened. But one thing she knew was that she was alone. Daisy started to cry. The sun was just about to drop into the mountains. Daisy walked back to the barn, holding Twurp.
She was very, very sad.

It was dark in the barn. Usually she had the comfort of her mother and brothers. She was frightened but she knew she had to try to be brave. She was afraid of the dark. Her mother always placed a jar of fireflies next to her bed so she would have a nightlight. But tonight was not like any other night. For the first time, Daisy was alone.

As the days passed, Daisy started to become accustomed to being alone. She would hunt for her food, mostly consisting of large bugs and lizards.

One day while Daisy was hunting, she came upon the shore where she last saw her family. She took a break from hunting. She lay in the tall grass, thinking of her mother and brothers. Her memories were happy.

Daisy heard some laughter coming from one of the grassy knolls. As curious as cats can be, she wanted to see what the laughter was about. She crawled quietly through the tall grass. As she peeked through the grass, she saw a family of bunnies having a picnic of carrot cake and apple cider.

Daisy continued to watch the family. After lunch the two brother bunnies jumped up and started running and tossing paper airplanes towards the sky. Daisy didn't want the bunnies to see her.

She lay motionless. But the bunnies, unaware of Daisy, ran closer and closer. And WHOMP they fell right on top of her. Startled, Daisy and the boys jumped up. At first the three looked at each other strangely. "What are you?" The younger bunny asked. "She's a cat," the older bunny replied.   "Your tail is funny looking. It's soooo long," the younger bunny said. Daisy quickly retorted, "You have long ears and they are floppy, too!"   "Hey! We have something in common," the older bunny said. "Bunnies and cats love to run. Let's race - bunnies against kitties!"

Daisy and the bunnies played all day. They eventually became exhausted. They sat along the shore. Daisy shared her story with her new friends. The boys liked Daisy and they also felt sorry for her. "You can stay with us," they said at the same time. At first, Daisy was hesitant. But the more she thought about it, she realized how much she wanted to be with a family.
She accepted their invitation.

The boys took Daisy to meet their mother, Monny Bunny who was resting in the shade under the tree where they had been picnicking. Monny Bunny thought Daisy was adorable. She agreed that Daisy should stay with them.

As time went by, Monny Bunny loved Daisy as if she were one of her own children.

One day Monny Bunny said, "I have a surprise for you, Daisy." Daisy and the bunny boys jumped up and down. They shouted, "WHAT IS IT? WHAT IS IT?" Monny Bunny handed Daisy a box tied with a shiny pink ribbon. Daisy carefully untied the ribbon and lifted the lid. Inside the box was a bunny suit that Monny Bunny had lovingly sewn for her. Daisy clapped her paws with joy. Everyone was so excited. The bunny boys danced around the room yelling for Daisy to try it on. And so she did. It was a perfect fit. "You look like us," the boys said. Daisy loved her new suit. Daisy gave Monny Bunny a huge hug and a great big kiss.

Daisy loved her new suit so much that she only took it off when Monny Bunny insisted that it needed to be washed. The bunny suit became her security blanket.

THE MAGIC SUIT

One day, while Daisy and the boys were playing hide and seek in the forest, it was Daisy's turn to hide. She was very competitive. She didn't like being found. She ventured deeper and deeper into the forest than she had ever gone before. She hid in the hollow of a large tree stump and waited for the bunny boys to find her. But they never came. It was getting late. Daisy decided to go home. As she walked through the forest nothing looked familiar. She realized that she was lost and tired. She decided to rest for a while on a nice mossy log. She started to think of her kitty family. It was such a long time since she had seen her mother and brothers. She missed them very much.

It was just about dark and there was still no sign of the boys. Daisy realized that her kitty sense was trying to tell her something. It was then that she noticed a small shimmering light. It was growing larger and coming closer and closer. Daisy became frightened. She felt she should run and hide, but she was very curious. She crouched down and became very, very still. The shimmering light grew brighter and larger. POOF! There was a large flash of light and shimmering fairy dust was everywhere. Daisy was captivated. All at once, floating in front of her very own eyes was a quite large, but sweet looking Bunny Fairy. Daisy could hardly believe what she saw. She had never seen anything magical before. Daisy whispered, "Who are you?" The Bunny Fairy spoke in a very soft voice, "I am the fairy of all bunnies. And I believe you must be Daisy. I have never seen a kitty in a bunny suit before," she added. Daisy just stood there in amazement; when she finally mustered up enough courage to say something - all that came out of her mouth was a teeny tiny squeak.

The Bunny Fairy sat down next to Daisy. Daisy spoke to her about her kitty family and how much she missed them. She told the Bunny Fairy about the love and warmth she received from her bunny family and about the bunny suit that Monny Bunny sewed for her, so that she could feel more comfortable around other bunnies. The Bunny Fairy stayed with Daisy through the night.

As morning came, the Bunny Fairy turned to Daisy and said, "I have been watching you ever since you became part of the bunny family. You have become independent and brave. I am here today because you are going to become magical." Daisy was confused. "But why me?" she asked. "Because you have the heart and spirit to make things right," replied the Bunny Fairy. The Bunny Fairy reached into her bag and pulled out a huge book of spells. "What is that?" Daisy asked. "It is all the magic that makes us bunnies. Thousands and thousands of years of magical spells were put together by all the bunny wizards."

The Bunny Fairy handed Daisy a glass bottle and she began to speak.

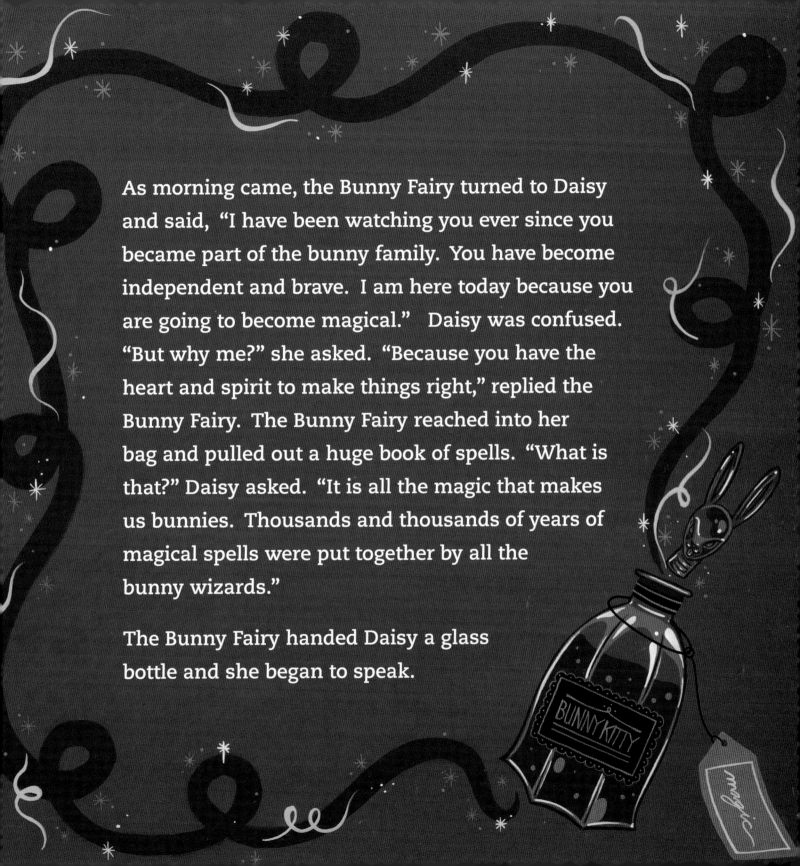

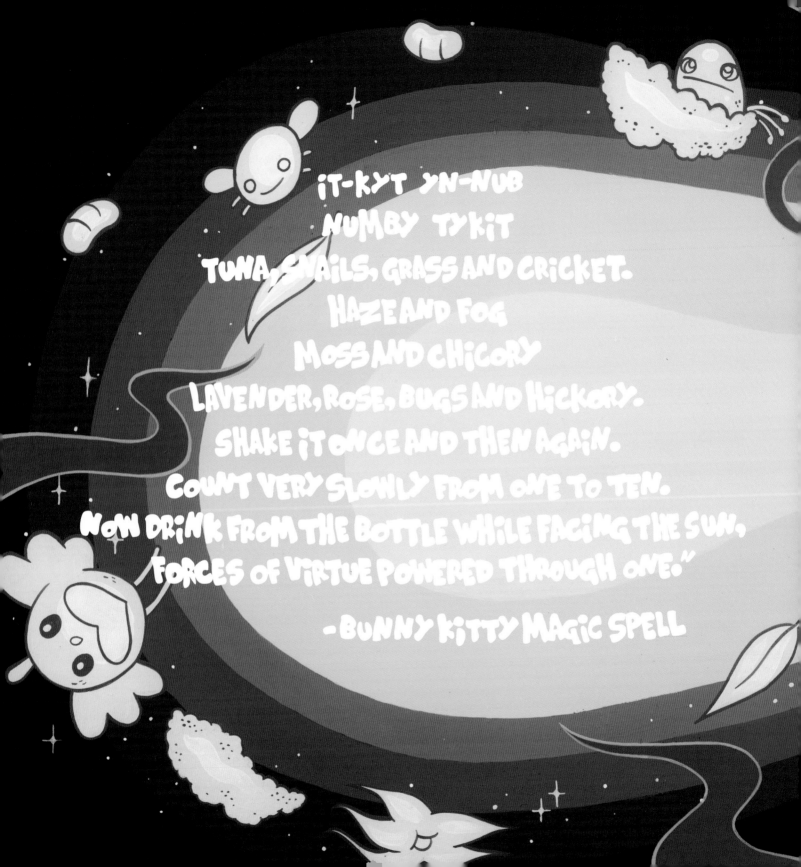

"IT-KYT YN-NUB
NUMBY TYKIT
TUNA, SNAILS, GRASS AND CRICKET.
HAZE AND FOG
MOSS AND CHICORY
LAVENDER, ROSE, BUGS AND HICKORY.
SHAKE IT ONCE AND THEN AGAIN.
COUNT VERY SLOWLY FROM ONE TO TEN.
NOW DRINK FROM THE BOTTLE WHILE FACING THE SUN,
FORCES OF VIRTUE POWERED THROUGH ONE."

-BUNNY KITTY MAGIC SPELL

And with a touch on the nose, a shock of energy ran through Daisy's little body. She could feel the magic all the way into her paws. "Now let us give it a try. Think of something and then reach into your bunny suit and pull it out," the Bunny Fairy said. Daisy thought of her favorite food and concentrated with all her might. She then reached into her suit and pulled out a huge salmon. "WOW!" she yelled.

The Bunny Fairy held Daisy close and said, "You are now Bunny Kitty."

The Bunny Fairy continued, "There are three very important things you need to know. One, all the magic of bunnies is now in your bunny suit. Two, you can only do GOOD magic with the suit. Three, the powers of the bunny suit won't work if you do not have it on."

The Bunny Fairy hugged Daisy and told her to be brave.
She pointed her in the direction of Monny Bunny's home.
And with a blink of an eye - the fairy vanished.

Daisy zipped off through the woods towards her bunny home. She was filled with excitement and could hardly wait to tell her bunny family what had just happened.

A BRAVE NEW WORLD

It was late morning when Daisy finally reached her bunny home. Everyone was so excited to see her. The boys were worried that they had lost her forever. Monny Bunny gave a sigh of relief. Daisy told the entire family what she went through and about the sweet Bunny Fairy she had met. Daisy told them about Bunny Kitty, the new name that was given to her by the Bunny Fairy. She told them all about her new powers and even demonstrated them by pulling out a big beautiful fresh baked carrot cake from her suit. Everyone cheered, "Hooray for Bunny Kitty!"

That entire day Bunny Kitty played with the boys. They had her do all kinds of magical tricks with her bunny suit. They were so happy and amazed to see the cat they once knew as Daisy turn into a magical Bunny Kitty.

That evening, back at home when the boys were asleep, Bunny Kitty finally had some time to talk to Monny Bunny alone. Monny Bunny spoke softly to Bunny Kitty, "You have grown up a lot in such a short amount of time. I know you are very curious to know what the world holds for you and where your real family is and what they are doing right now." Bunny Kitty's eyes filled with tears. "I want to see them again" She sniffled. "I want to be brave and look for them in the city. I know I can handle such an adventure now." Monny Bunny agreed and they spoke about the city and what good and bad things it had to offer. It was Bunny Kitty's decision that she would leave for the city in the morning. Monny Bunny held Bunny Kitty close and whispered into her ear, "You will always be my little Daisy."

The next morning came and everyone felt somber. Monny Bunny had told the boys that Bunny Kitty would be leaving for new adventures in the city. Even though everyone was sad, they were very supportive of Bunny Kitty's decision.

Monny Bunny packed Bunny Kitty her favorite sardine and turnip squares and other goodies for the long trip to the city.

It was time for Bunny Kitty to leave. The ferry would be coming soon and she could not afford to miss it again.

Bunny Kitty and her bunny family set off towards the riverbed in silence. The ferry was already at the dock when they reached the river. The boys were clinging to Monny Bunny's legs. They were crying because they loved Bunny Kitty very much and they didn't want to see her go. Bunny Kitty said, "I'll be alright. This isn't good-bye forever. We'll meet again - I promise."

"All aboard!" the captain yelled. Bunny Kitty ran into her bunny family's arms. They took turns saying something nice to each other and touched noses. Bunny Kitty then turned to the ferry and jumped aboard. "Remember, we'll see each other again!" she shouted. Monny yelled back, "Show them what you are made of!"As the ferry left the dock, Bunny Kitty waved to her bunny family until they were out of sight.

Bunny Kitty's eyes were wide with excitement. She had no idea where to start looking for her family, but nothing would keep her from trying.

She held her little birdie, Twurp, in her hands and whispered to him, "This time I didn't forget you."

TO BE CONTINUED

BE BRAVE

ABOUT:
DAVE "PERSUE" ROSS

Descended from a line of acclaimed artists, Dave "Persue" Ross continues family tradition and is recognized by his peers as a true artistic pioneer. With an energetic, illustrative style, his technical ability and poise as a young artist in the 1980's quickly earned him the respect of his contemporaries throughout the world. Persue shifted his focus from commercial work to his own projects, and relocated to New York City in 2014. His background as a graphic artist, designer, and muralist has equipped him with the wisdom and skills needed to bring Bunny Kitty to the world."

ABOUT:
DIANE 'MONNY' SATENSTEIN

Diane "Monny" Satenstein grew up in New York City and spent her younger years competing as an award-winning equestrian. She studied drama in her twenties, and spent time acting on stage in Manhattan. A loving mother of six children and eleven grandchildren, Diane's seemingly endless supply of love for her fellow humans afforded her a natural transition into devoting her later years to Social work. She received a Bachelor of Arts in Sociology. She enjoyed spending her free time reading, going to the movies, and attending museum exhibitions. Diane was goofy, compassionate, cultured, and intelligent, and we miss her deeply.